Topic: Interpersonal Skills   **Subtopic:** Celebrating Differences

Notes to Parents and Teachers:

As a child becomes more familiar reading books, it is important for them to rely on and use reading strategies more independently to help figure out words they do not know.

REMEMBER: PRAISE IS A GREAT MOTIVATOR!

Here are some praise points for beginning readers:

• I saw you get your mouth ready to say the first letter of that word.
• I like the way you used the picture to help you figure out that word.
• I noticed that you saw some sight words you knew how to read!

Book Ends for the Reader!

Here are some reminders before reading the text:

• Point to each word you read to make it match what you say.

• Use the picture for help.

• Look at and say the first letter sound of the word.

• Look for sight words that you know how to read in the story.

• Think about the story to see what word might make sense.

Words to Know Before You Read

ducks

friend

girl

help

like

no

play

yes

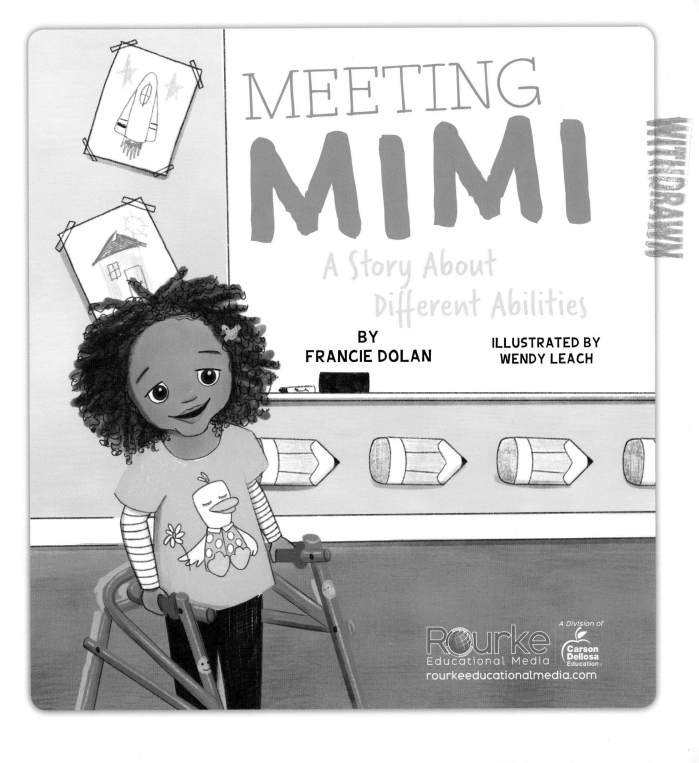

"I am Mimi," the new girl said.

4

"I like jokes. I like ducks. I have a disability. And, I like questions!"

Everyone was quiet.

Everyone stared.

But soon, everyone had questions.

"Have you read this?"

"Yes, I love that story!"

"Can I try your walker?"

"No, I need it to help me walk."

"Have you ever built a rocket?"

"No, but I want to help."

"Can you lift things?"

"Yes, my arms are strong!"

"Can I help you carry?"

"Yes, thank you!"

14

"Do you like beans?"

"No, not really."

"Will you use the stairs?"

"No, I'll take the ramp."

"Can you play outside with us?"

"Yes, I love recess!"

At circle time, Mimi raised her hand.

"Now I have a question. What is a crate of ducks?"

"A box of quackers!"

No one was quiet. No one stared. Everyone laughed with their new friend Mimi.

Book Ends for the Reader

I know...

1. Tell three things you know about Mimi.
2. How does Mimi's walker help her?
3. Why does Mimi use the ramp instead of the stairs?

I think...

1. How does Mimi feel when her classmates stare at her?
2. How does Mimi feel when her classmates ask her to play?
3. What question would you ask Mimi?

Book Ends for the Reader

What happened in this book?

Look at each picture and talk about what happened in the story.

About the Author

Francie Dolan is a writer from Columbus, Ohio. Her favorite animal is a moose. Her favorite vegetable is carrots. She is very glad we live in a world where everyone is different.

About the Illustrator

Wendy Leach is an illustrator from Kansas with a love for art supplies! When she is not illustrating, she can be found in the aisles of her local art shop.

Library of Congress PCN Data

Meeting Mimi (A Story About Different Abilities) / Francie Dolan
(Playing and Learning Together)
ISBN 978-1-73160-586-3 (hard cover)(alk. paper)
ISBN 978-1-73160-422-4 (soft cover)
ISBN 978-1-73160-639-6 (e-Book)
ISBN 978-1-73160-659-4 (ePub)
Library of Congress Control Number: 2018967349

Rourke Educational Media
Printed in the United States of America,
North Mankato, Minnesota

www.rourkeeducationalmedia.com

Edited by: Kim Thompson
Layout by: Kathy Walsh
Cover and interior illustrations by: Wendy Leach